Sun is Falling

Night is Calling

by Laura Leuck · illustrated by Ora Eitan

SIMON & SCHUSTER BOOKS FOR YOUNG READERS
Published by Simon & Schuster
New York   London   Toronto   Sydney   Tokyo   Singapore

SIMON & SCHUSTER BOOKS FOR YOUNG READERS
Simon & Schuster Building, Rockefeller Center
1230 Avenue of the Americas, New York, New York 10020
Text copyright © 1994 by Laura Leuck. Illustrations
copyright © 1994 by Ora Eitan. All rights reserved
including the right of reproduction in whole or in part in
any form. SIMON & SCHUSTER BOOKS FOR YOUNG READERS
is a trademark of Simon & Schuster.
Designed by Lucille Chomowicz.
The text for this book is set in Breughel 55.
The illustrations were done in gouache.
Manufactured in the United States of America
10 9 8 7 6 5 4 3 2 1

Library of Congress Cataloging-in-Publication Data
Leuck, Laura. Sun is falling, night is calling / by Laura
Leuck; illustrated by Ora Eitan. Summary: Rhyming
text and illustrations describe the day's end as a mother
puts her child to bed. [1. Bedtime—Fiction.
2. Night—Fiction.   3. Mother and child—Fiction.]
I. Eitan, Ora, 1940-   ill. II. Title. PZ7.L5715Ni
1993 [E]—dc20 93-22837 CIP
ISBN 0-671-86940-X

For my family —L.L.

To my children,
Danny and Noa —O.E.

Day is ending,
so is play.

Mama says,
"Now toys away."

Day is done,
the sun is falling.

Mama says,
"The night is calling."

Dusk's around us,
night is near.

Mama says,
"Come snuggle here."

Twilight falls
as six bells chime.

Mama says,
"It's story time."

Night is coming,
rest is near.

Mama says,
"To bed, my dear."

Night is coming,
won't be long.

Mama sings
a gentle song.

Day has ended,
dark already.

Mama says,
"Now here's your teddy."

Night has come,
the moon is peeping.

Mama says,
"It's time for sleeping."

Night has come
with crickets humming.

Mama says,
"Sweet dreams are coming."

Night has come
with moonlit skies.

Mama says,
"Now close your eyes."

Night has come
with stars above.

Mama says,
"Good night, my love."